D1180743

This LADYBIRD CLASSIC
belongs to

....

A History of the Author

Louisa May Alcott was an American novelist born in 1832. Her family suffered much hardship and the story of *Little Women* is partly based on her own experiences. She originally wrote novels for adults, but the success of *Little Women* encouraged her to focus on writing for children.

Chapter illustrations by Valeria Valenza

A catalogue record for this book is available from the British Library

Published by Ladybird Books Ltd
80 Strand London WC2R 0RL
A Penguin Company

001

© Ladybird Books Ltd MMXIV

ISBN: 978-0-72327-087-4

Printed in China

LADYBIRD 🐞 CLASSICS

Little Women

by Louisa May Alcott

Retold by Joan Collins
Illustrated by Chiara Fedele

Contents

CHAPTER ONE

Meg, Jo, Beth and Amy

'CHRISTMAS WON'T BE Christmas without any presents,' grumbled Jo, stretching out her long legs on the hearth rug.

'It's dreadful to be poor!' sighed Meg, looking down at her shabby dress.

'I don't think it's fair for some girls to have everything and other girls nothing at all,' added little Amy with a sniff.

'We've got Father and Mother and each other,' said Beth contentedly, from her corner.

The firelight flickered over the faces of the four sisters as they sat knitting in the cosy room as the December snow fell gently outside.

But Jo said sadly, 'We haven't got Father, and shan't have him for a very long time.' The girls' father, Mr March, was too old to fight in the American Civil War, so he had volunteered to be an army chaplain. The girls were very proud of him.

It was going to be a hard winter for the men in the army. The girls' mother, whom they called Marmee, thought they ought not to spend any money on presents for themselves that Christmas. 'We should give up something, too,' she had said.

The girls were disappointed. They had looked forward to spending their hard-earned pocket money. Jo had

planned to buy a favourite book, Beth some piano music and Amy, the artistic one, drawing pencils.

'We do deserve some fun,' said Jo. 'After all, we work hard enough.'

'I know I do,' said Meg, the pretty one, who was sixteen. She was a nursery governess to a family of naughty children. Jo, the fifteen-year-old tomboy, went every day to look after her cross, elderly aunt. Shy Beth, thirteen, stayed at home. Amy, eleven and the youngest, was still at school.

The clock struck six, and Beth put her mother's slippers by the fire to warm.

'They're nearly worn out. Marmee needs a new pair,' said Jo.

The girls' faces lit up. Suddenly they knew what to buy with their Christmas money!

'Glad to find you so merry, girls!' said a voice from the doorway. It was Marmee, in her old cloak and plain bonnet, the dearest mother in the world.

Mrs March took off her wet things, put on her warm slippers and prepared for the happiest hour of the day. 'Sit down,' she said. 'I've got a treat for you!' And she patted her pocket.

'A letter from Father!' they all cried.

The letter was cheerful. Only at the end did their father show how much he missed his daughters:

'When I come back, I shall be fonder and prouder than ever of my little women.'

The letter brought tears to the girls' eyes, and they made some resolutions. Jo promised not to be so wild, Amy not to be so selfish, and Meg not to be so vain. Quiet Beth said nothing, but began to knit with all her might!

Mrs March smiled at her daughters.

'Do you remember the game of Pilgrim's Progress you played when you were little?' she asked. 'You climbed from the basement, which was the City of Destruction, all the way up to the Celestial City, which was the attic, carrying your burdens.'

'I liked the place where the burdens fell off!' said Meg.

'I liked the cake and milk at the top!' said Amy. 'I wish we weren't too old to play it now.'

'That is a game you play all your lives,' said Marmee wisely. 'See how far you can get on the journey before Father comes home!'

'But what are our burdens?' asked the girls.

'I think you've just told me about them,' said Marmee. 'Only Beth hasn't mentioned hers. I think perhaps she hasn't got any.'

'Mine are dishes and dusters and envying girls with nice pianos, and being afraid of people!' confessed Beth.

Before they went to bed, the girls sang carols together. The quiet, happy music was their Christmas lullaby.

CHAPTER TWO

A Merry Christmas

WHEN THE GIRLS ran down to
breakfast on Christmas morning, Marmee
wasn't there to greet them.

'There was a poor creetur come
a-begging, and your ma went straight off to
see what was needed,' said Hannah. Hannah
had been with them since they were babies,
and was part of the family by now.

The girls put their mother's presents on

the table and waited eagerly for her return.
At last the door banged, and in she came.

'There was a woman nearby with a little
newborn baby,' she said. 'She has six children
huddled in one bed to keep warm. They have
no food or fire. Will you give them your
breakfast as a Christmas present?'

The girls piled up buckwheat cakes and
muffins on plates. Hannah took an armful
of wood and some blankets, and they set off.

Marmee took them to a bare, miserable
room, where there was a sick mother and
hungry children crowded together under
an old quilt.

'It's good angels come to help us!' cried
the poor woman, hugging her baby.

'Funny angels, in hoods and mittens!'
laughed Jo, as they fed the children and
Hannah built a fire.

Back at home, they gave Marmee
her new slippers and had bread and milk
for breakfast.

Jo had written a Christmas play. It was an 'operatic tragedy' about a witch, a villain and a pair of lovers. The props and costumes were all homemade, and the performance was held in the old barn next to the house.

Jo played all the male roles, Meg was the witch, and Amy the golden-haired heroine. Beth played all the minor parts, and kept forgetting her lines.

All went well until the heroine's dress got caught, just as she was eloping from a 'tower' of piled-up chairs. Both she and the tower came crashing to the floor. A pair of leather boots waved wildly in the ruins, and a golden head appeared, shrieking, 'I told you so!'

At the end, there was loud applause from the 'dress circle', which was a cot-bed. Then Hannah came in to call everyone in to supper.

The girls' eyes opened wide when they

saw the magnificent spread. There were two kinds of ice cream, cake, fruit, and sweets, all decorated with hothouse flowers.

Their next-door neighbour, rich old Mr Laurence, had been *their* 'good angel'. He had heard of the morning's doings, and sent 'a few trifles'. It certainly made up for the bread-and-milk breakfast.

'That boy put it into his head!' cried Jo, who had met the old man's grandson, Laurie, when he had returned their runaway cat. He was normally inside, kept hard at work at lessons with his tutor.

'I mean to make friends with that boy one day,' Jo decided. 'I know he needs some fun!'

'I wish we could send some of these flowers to Father,' said Beth wistfully. 'I'm afraid he isn't having as merry a Christmas as we are!'

CHAPTER THREE

Burdens

'I WISH IT were Christmas all the time!'
said Jo, when the holidays were over.

Everyone seemed out of sorts at
breakfast that morning. Beth had a
headache, Jo had broken her shoelace,
Amy had not done her homework. Poor
Mrs March was trying to write a letter
amidst all the confusion.

At last, the girls set off to begin their

day's work – to take up their 'burdens'.

Jo's burden was fetching and carrying for crotchety old Aunt March, who was lame and needed help at home. Jo disliked the work but she loved the large library. The moment Aunt March took a nap, Jo hurried off to the dim room and curled up in an armchair to read.

But always, when she got to the most interesting part, a shrill voice would call, 'Josy-phine!' and she would have to go and wash the poodle, feed the parrot, wind wool or read something dull and tedious to her aunt.

Meg was old enough to remember the pleasant life at home before their father had lost all his money trying to help a friend. It was hard for her to have to work now, and especially hard to work for the rich King family.

But that day there was trouble. Mrs King was crying, Mr King was shouting, and the

girls were silent. The eldest son had done something to disgrace the family. Perhaps money wasn't everything, Meg thought.

Beth had her lessons at home and helped Hannah. She spent quiet days alone, busy with chores or caring tenderly for her three kittens. She also had six battered old dolls that she loved.

Beth's secret sorrow was that she could not have music lessons. She practised patiently on the jingly old piano, with its yellow keys that would never keep in tune, hoping that 'one day I'll get my music, if I'm good!'

Amy's burden was her rather flat nose. She wished it were 'aristocratic' and she drew page after page of handsome noses to comfort herself.

Amy was popular with her school friends. They admired her little airs and graces and the long words she used (not always the right ones!). But her vanity

was kept in check because she had to wear her cousin's cast-off dresses. They offended Amy's artistic taste!

That evening, the girls brought back tales of their day's activities. Marmee listened, gently guiding them to see how lucky they were in their happy family life, even though they could not have everything they wanted.

CHAPTER FOUR

The Laurence Boy

THE MARCH FAMILY'S house was
separated by a hedge from the Laurences'
stately stone mansion. The Laurence
house was a lonely place; almost no one
but the old gentleman and his grandson
went in and out.

Jo imagined the house to be a palace
of delights with nobody there to enjoy
them. And for a long time she had wanted

to make friends with the 'Laurence boy'.

One snowy afternoon, while she was outside, she saw old Mr Laurence drive off. At an upstairs window, she saw a dark curly head leaning on a thin hand.

Jo tossed a snowball up.

Laurie's face brightened at once and he opened the window.

'You need some company!' said Jo cheerfully.

'So I do!' Laurie replied. 'Would you come up?'

'I must ask Marmee first,' Jo said and ran off into her house.

She returned carrying Beth's kittens and a dish of Meg's blancmange, decorated with flowers from Amy's pet geranium.

'Everyone wanted to do something!' she said. She swept the hearth and plumped up the cushions to make the room cosy.

Jo made Laurie laugh with tales of Aunt March and her parrot that spoke

Spanish. Laurie wanted to know all about Jo's family. He often watched them at night, gathered round their mother in the lamplight. Laurie had no mother. Jo could tell he was lonely.

'I wish you'd come over, instead of peeping,' she said. 'We'd have such a jolly time!'

When old Mr Laurence came back, Jo found that he was not nearly as frightening as she had imagined. He told her he had been a friend of her grandfather, and showed her his splendid library.

'What have you been doing to this boy of mine?' he asked her over tea.

'Trying to cheer him up!' Jo said. 'I think he could do with some young company.'

Mr Laurence watched the two laughing and talking together. 'She's right,' he thought. 'The lad is lonely. I'll see what these girls can do for him.' He liked Jo's blunt ways, and she seemed to understand the boy.

A little later, Laurie played on the grand piano. Jo wished Beth could hear him.

When she went home, with an armful of hothouse flowers, she told her family all about her afternoon.

'I was thinking about Pilgrim's Progress,' said Beth dreamily. 'When Christian got up the steep hill, he came to the Palace Beautiful. Maybe the house over there is going to be our Palace Beautiful.'

'We've got to get past the lions first!' said Jo.

CHAPTER FIVE

Beth Finds the Palace Beautiful

THE BIG HOUSE did prove a Palace
Beautiful, though Beth found it very hard
to pass the lions. For her, the biggest lion
was old Mr Laurence. But even Beth
was not shy with Laurie. His tutor,
Mr Brooke, complained that Laurie was
always playing truant now and running
over to the Marches.

'Never mind!' said his grandfather.

'He deserves a holiday, and he won't come to any harm over there.'

At the Laurence house, Jo had the freedom of the library, Meg loved the hothouse, and Amy copied the pictures. But Beth was too shy to touch the grand piano. Mr Laurence noticed this. One day he asked Mrs March if any of her girls would like to come over and practise – 'to keep the piano in tune'.

'They needn't see anybody,' he said slyly. 'I'm always shut up in my study in the evenings, and there are no servants about. But if the girls don't care to, never mind.'

A little hand slipped timidly into his. 'Oh, sir, they do care, very much!' said Beth.

Mr Laurence looked down. Beth's blue eyes reminded him of his granddaughter who had died and his heart softened even more.

After that, Beth came to play the piano nearly every day and he often left his study door open to hear the sweet music that she made.

Beth decided to embroider a pair of slippers with pansies for Mr Laurence, as a thank-you present. Imagine her joy and surprise when, the next day, a beautiful little cabinet piano was delivered for 'Miss Elizabeth March'. It had belonged to Mr Laurence's granddaughter. With it was a note:

'Heart's-ease is my favourite flower.
Your grateful friend and humble servant,
James Laurence.'

'You'll have to go over and thank him,' teased Jo, never dreaming Beth would have the courage.

But she surprised them all. She marched straight over to the house, climbed up on Mr Laurence's knee, and kissed him.

'I do believe the world is coming to an end!' Meg gasped.

And Beth was never afraid of Mr Laurence again.

CHAPTER SIX

Jo Meets her Dark Angel

'GIRLS, WHERE ARE you going?' asked
Amy, coming into their room one Saturday
afternoon and finding Meg and Jo ready
to go out.

'Never you mind!' answered Jo sharply.

Amy's feelings were hurt. She had been
feeling very left out of things lately.

It turned out that Laurie was taking Meg
and Jo to see a play. Amy wanted to go, too.

She began to cry, but Jo refused to take her. 'It would spoil everything!' she said.

'You'll be sorry for this, Jo March!' called Amy over the banisters, as the girls went out.

'Fiddlesticks!' said Jo, slamming the door.

When they got home, Amy was sitting in the parlour, reading. She did not ask a single question about the play. Jo was suspicious.

She went upstairs and looked round her room to see what mischief Amy had done, but everything was in order.

Next day, however, Jo discovered that a little book of fairy stories she had written was missing. She had worked on the book lovingly for a year, and it was her only copy.

Jo pounced on Amy. 'You've got it!' she said.

'Scold as much as you like, you'll never see it again! I burned it up!' cried Amy triumphantly. 'I said I'd pay you back!'

Jo turned pale and shook Amy till her teeth chattered. 'I'll never forgive you, never!'

Even when Amy said she was sorry, Jo would not make friends.

As she kissed Jo good night, Marmee whispered, 'Don't let the sun go down on your anger, dear. Forgive each other and begin again tomorrow.'

'She doesn't deserve to be forgiven!' said Jo gruffly.

Next day was the last day of winter skating. To cheer herself up, Jo went down to the river with Laurie. They had promised to take Amy skating before the ice broke up, but Jo was still cross and went without her.

Amy ran after them, meaning to tell Jo how truly sorry she was. Jo saw her on the bank, struggling with her skates, but took no notice.

Laurie had skated ahead to see if the ice was safe. 'Keep near the bank!' he called. 'It's dangerous in the middle!'

But Amy did not hear him. Jo could see that Amy hadn't heard but her little demon

of a temper whispered, 'Let her take care
of herself!'

So Amy skated out onto the smoother ice.

Suddenly the ice broke. Amy disappeared.

The next few moments were a nightmare
for Jo. At last, she and Laurie managed to pull
Amy out of the icy water, but she knew that
the accident was her fault.

When Amy was safely home, Jo confessed
to Marmee. 'It's my dreadful temper!' she cried.

Marmee put her arms round the sobbing
Jo and told her a secret. 'Mine used to be just
like it. I've been trying to control it for forty
years!' And she explained how their father had
taught her to be patient. She talked lovingly
to Jo about forgiveness.

Jo went up to look at Amy in bed and
thought how dreadful it would have been if
that golden head had been swept away for
ever under the ice. Amy opened her eyes.
Her arms went round Jo, and everything was
forgotten in one sisterly kiss.

CHAPTER SEVEN

Meg Goes to Vanity Fair

ONE APRIL AFTERNOON, Meg was excitedly packing her best things to go on a visit to her friend Sallie Moffat. The sisters all gathered round her, offering to lend her their treasures.

Meg was doubtful about her old party dress of white muslin. 'It will have to do,' she sighed.

'Never mind! You always look like

an angel in white,' said Amy, looking enviously at Meg's silk stockings, pretty fan and two pairs of gloves.

The Moffats were fashionable folk, and Meg was dazzled by the splendour of their house. They were kind, and gave her what they called 'a good time' – shopping, entertaining and paying calls.

On the evening of the party, Meg was still feeling miserable about her dress, until a box of beautiful flowers arrived from Laurie. She generously divided them up into posies for all her friends. Then she happily fastened roses to the neck of her white dress, which did not seem half so shabby now.

Meg enjoyed herself that evening. She heard one of the guests, Major Lincoln, ask who 'the fresh little girl with the beautiful eyes' was, and she was asked to sing.

Then everything was spoiled.

Meg overheard Mrs Moffat and some

of her friends gossiping about the flowers
Laurie had sent.

'It would be a grand thing for one of
those girls! Sallie says the old man quite
dotes on them.'

'Mrs M has made her plans, I dare say!'

'Would she mind if we lent her a dress
for Thursday? That dowdy muslin is all she
has got.'

'We'll ask young Laurence, as a favour to
her,' said Mrs Moffat.

Meg was horrified to hear them speak
so of her mother, and of the March family's
innocent friendship with Laurie.

Next day, she was told of the invitation
to 'Mr Laurence'.

'It's very kind of you,' she said
mischievously, 'but I'm afraid he won't come.'

'Why not?'

'He's too old — nearly seventy!'

'We meant the *young* Mr Laurence,
of course!'

'Oh, he's only a *boy*!' laughed Meg.

Laurie did come, encouraged by the March family, who wanted to know how Meg looked. But he was disappointed. She had allowed the Moffat girls to dress her up like a doll. She wore a low-cut blue silk dress of Sallie's and a pair of high-heeled blue silk boots. They had frizzled her hair and given her cheeks a dusting of powder and rouge.

'Don't you like it?' said Meg, waving her plumy fan.

'I don't like fuss and feathers,' said Laurie honestly.

Meg stalked away and tried to cool her flushed cheeks. Major Lincoln came by with his mother. 'They are making a fool of that girl,' he said. 'I wanted you to see her, but they have spoiled her entirely.'

Meg begged Laurie not to tell Marmee how she had behaved and looked. 'I want to tell her myself,' she said.

And she did confess to Marmee, and told her about the gossip she had overheard. 'Do you have 'plans' for us, Marmee?' asked Meg.

'Yes, my dear. But mine are different from Mrs Moffat's. I am ambitious for my girls, but not for them to marry rich men just because they are rich. Better to be happy old maids than unhappy wives!'

CHAPTER EIGHT

Summer Doings

WHEN THE SUMMER holidays came, the girls begged Marmee to be allowed to do exactly as they liked for a week, and be free of chores. As Marmee foresaw, this was a disaster.

Meg chose to alter (and spoil) her dresses by trimming them up like Sallie Moffat's. Amy sat in the garden in her best dress, drawing, and soon became bored with her own company. Jo read all day and got a headache. Beth forgot to feed her canary, Pip, and it died.

On the last day, both Marmee and Hannah went out, to see how the girls would manage without them.

Jo decided to give a lunch party, and invited Laurie. Jo's choice of lobster, asparagus and salad, with homemade bread, followed by strawberries and cream sprinkled with sugar sounded wonderful. But the meal went wrong right down to the dessert. Laurie took a mouthful, gulped, and chewed on manfully.

'What's wrong?' cried Jo.

'Salt instead of sugar, and the cream's sour!' gasped Meg. They all burst out laughing, and the meal ended with bread and butter, cold meat, and fun.

'Now you see what happens when everyone thinks only of herself,' said Marmee on her return with Hannah.

'Don't you think it's better when each of us takes her share of daily duties?'

'We do, Mother, we do,' chorused the girls.

'From now on we'll work like bees,' said Jo. 'I'm going to learn plain cooking for my holiday task!'

Laurie had guests visiting from England during the summer, and the high spot of the season was a whole day's boating picnic to entertain them.

A quiet observer at the picnic might have noticed that Laurie's tutor, Mr Brooke, paid special attention to Meg. Laurie noticed this himself, and mentioned it to Jo. She, as the protector of the family, was furious at the idea!

Chapter Nine

A Telegram

'NOVEMBER IS THE most disagreeable month of the year,' said Meg one winter afternoon, as she and her sisters looked out at the frostbitten garden.

'Two nice things are going to happen right away!' exclaimed Beth. 'Marmee is coming down the street, and Laurie is tramping through the garden. He promised to take us for a drive.'

The two came in, Marmee with her usual question: 'Is there a letter from Father? It's not like him to be so late.'

A sharp ring of the doorbell interrupted her, and Hannah came in with a letter. 'It's one of them horrible telegraph things,' she said.

At the word 'telegraph', Mrs March snatched it, read the two lines it contained, and dropped back into her chair with a white face. Jo read it aloud, in a frightened voice:

'Blank Hospital, Washington
Mrs March,
Your husband is very ill. Come at once.
S Hale'

The room was still. The day darkened outside, and the whole world seemed to change. 'It may be too late – oh, children, help me to bear it!' said Mrs March, in a voice they never forgot.

Hannah was the first to recover.

'The Lord keep the dear man! I won't waste time cryin', but git your things ready right away, ma'am!'

The girls hurried to help Marmee to pack. Laurie was sent out to send a telegram saying Marmee would come at once. He was also to leave a note at Aunt March's. Jo knew the money for the journey would have to be borrowed from Aunt March, and she wished she could do something to help.

Then old Mr Laurence came. There was nothing he did not offer, but Mrs March would not hear of it – she knew he was too old and frail to travel – so he left.

A few minutes later, as Meg was carrying a pair of overshoes in one hand and a cup of tea in the other, Mr Brooke came in the door. He offered *his* services to escort Mrs March to Washington. Mr Laurence had some important business for him to attend there, he said.

Meg dropped the overshoes and nearly spilt the cup of tea, putting out her hands to him in gratitude, and John Brooke felt amply repaid.

Everything was arranged. The money came from Aunt March, with a note saying she'd always said their father was a fool to go. Jo saw her mother bite her lips, and knew how she felt. Suddenly, Jo rushed out.

When she came back, looking very strange, she laid a roll of bills on her mother's lap. Twenty-five dollars!

'It's my contribution to helping Father and seeing him home safely,' she said.

'Where did you get it?' everyone asked.

Jo took off her bonnet. Her long, thick hair had all been cut short.

'This crop is so comfortable I know I'll never miss it!' she said. 'The barber's wife gave me a lock to keep, but I'll give it to you, Marmee.'

Marmee took it and put it away

carefully. She only said, 'Thank you, dear,' but something in her face made the girls change the subject.

That night, a quiet figure glided from bed to bed, looking at her sleeping daughters. As she lifted the curtain and looked into the dreary night, the moon broke through, as if to whisper, 'There is always light behind the clouds.'

CHAPTER TEN

Letters

IN THE MORNING, Hannah cheered the girls up briskly and made coffee as a breakfast treat. As they set off for work, there was no Marmee waving goodbye. But Beth had not forgotten them. Her rosy face smiled as she waved to them from the window.

'That's my Beth!' said Jo.

Good news of their father comforted

the sisters. Mr Brooke sent regular despatches.

The girls wrote letters of their own to their mother. Jo's were comic:

'Everyone is so desperately good, it's like living in a nest of turtledoves! You'd laugh to see Meg head the table and try to be motherish!'

Amy complained:

'Laurie is not as respeckful as he ought to be now I am almost in my teens, he calls me Chick.'

Hannah was blunt:

'The old gentleman sends heaps of things and means wal, and it aint my place to say nothin. I send my duty to Mr March and hope he's seen the last of his Pewmonia.'

Mr Laurence's letter was to the point:

'Dear Madam,

The little girls are all well. Pray make Brooke useful, and draw on me for funds. Don't let your husband want for anything. Thank God he is mending.

Your sincere friend and servant,

James Laurence.'

CHAPTER ELEVEN

Dark Days

ONE DAY, BETH went to see the poor
family they had all visited at Christmas.
She came back sadly. The baby had died
of scarlet fever in Beth's lap. Now Beth had
a headache and a sore throat and felt ill.

'If only Mother were at home!' cried Jo.

Jo and Meg had both had scarlet fever,
but Amy had not, so she was packed off to
Aunt March's.

Beth did have the fever, and was very sick. She talked in a broken voice and played on the quilt as if it were her piano. She did not know anybody, and cried for Marmee. But Mr March was still very ill, and Marmee could not come home.

One day, the doctor looked at Beth for a long time. 'If Mrs March can leave her husband, she should be sent for,' he said gravely.

Jo rushed out of the house to send a telegram, and ran full tilt into Laurie.

'Beth mustn't die! She's my conscience!' Jo sobbed wildly.

'I don't think she will die,' said Laurie, soothing her. 'She's so good, and we all love her so much.' Then he told Jo that he had already telegraphed, and that Marmee was on her way.

'Bless you, Laurie!' Jo cried.

The joyous whisper 'Mother's coming!' ran through the house. The hours dragged

by, and night came. At two o'clock Jo bent over Beth's bed. Beth's face was still and pale. Jo thought she was dying.

'Goodbye, Beth, goodbye!' she whispered.

Then Hannah came. 'The fever's turned!' she cried. 'She's sleeping natural!'

When the doctor came that morning, he confirmed the good news: Beth was over the worst.

'If only Marmee would come,' said Jo. Suddenly there was a sound of bells at the door, a cry from Hannah, and Laurie's voice: 'Girls! She's come! She's come!'

CHAPTER TWELVE

Problems

THERE ARE NO words to describe the
reunion. When Beth woke from that long,
healing sleep, the first thing she saw was
her mother's face.

Laurie went to give the good news
to Amy, who had learned much at Aunt
March's. When her mother came to see
her, Amy was wearing a pretty ring that
Aunt March had given her. 'It's to remind

me not to be selfish,' Amy said.

Jo had her problems, too. She resented John Brooke's relationship with Meg. John had fallen in love with Meg and wanted to marry her.

But Meg was still very young, and not sure of her own feelings. She was confused and upset when John proposed.

Aunt March came to the house and told Meg she would leave her nothing in her will if she married a poor man!

Meg defended Mr Brooke bravely. 'I shall marry whom I please, Aunt March. And you can leave your money to anyone you like!'

'I couldn't help overhearing, Meg,' said John, who had come by to get an umbrella he had left. 'So you do care for me a bit!'

'Yes, John,' said Meg meekly, hiding her face in his waistcoat. 'I didn't realize how much, before!'

CHAPTER THIRTEEN

Christmas Once More

BEFORE THE CHRISTMAS dinner
came the presents. The best one of all
was announced by Laurie at the door:

'Here's another Christmas present for
the March family!'

A tall man, muffled up to his ears,
came in, leaning on the arm of another
tall man. Everyone rushed to hug him.

'Hush! Remember Beth!' Marmee

cried – but it was too late. The door flew open, and little Beth, in her red wrapper, flew straight into her father's arms.

There never was such a Christmas dinner. After it, Mr March looked round at his little women. Meg was more womanly, Jo less boyish, Amy more thoughtful of others, and Beth not so shy.

'What are you thinking, Beth?' asked Jo.

'I read in Pilgrim's Progress how, after many troubles, Christian and Hopeful came into pleasant meadows,' Beth said, 'and they sang this song. It's Father's favourite.'

Beth went to her piano and sang in her sweet voice:

'He that is down need fear no fall,
He that is low, no pride,
He that is humble ever shall
Have God to be his guide.'

Father and Mother sat together, while Amy sketched the lovers, Meg and John. Beth talked to her old friend, Mr Laurence,

while Jo lounged on her favourite seat. Laurie, smiling, leaned on the back of Jo's chair.

So grouped, the curtain falls on Meg, Jo, Beth, and Amy. Whether it ever rises again depends on the reception given to the first act of the domestic drama called *Little Women*.

Collect more fantastic
LADYBIRD CLASSICS

Alice in Wonderland
9781409311232

Oliver Twist
9781409311256

Treasure Island
9781409311287

BLACK BEAUTY
9781409311249

GULLIVER'S Travels
9781409311270

The Secret Garden
9781409311263

A Christmas Carol
9781409312215

Peter Pan
9781409312222

The Three Musketeers
9781409313557

THE WIND IN THE WILLOWS
9781409313564

Heidi
9781409313571

The Jungle Book
9781409313588

The Railway Children
9780723270867

Little Women
9780723270874